Christmas in Tennessee

KAYLA LOWE

Want a free book? Sign up to my newsletter to get my award-winning book for free! www.authorkaylalowe.com

<u>Sweet Honey by the Sea</u>

<u>The Beekeeper's Secret (Book 1)</u>
<u>A Royal Honeycomb (Book 2)</u>
<u>Bees in Blossom (Book 3)</u>
<u>Honeyed Kisses (Book 4)</u>
<u>Blooming Forever (Book 5)</u>

<u>Strawberry Beach Series</u>

<u>Beachside Lessons (Book 1)</u>
<u>Beachside Lessons (Book 2)</u>
<u>Beachside Lessons (Book 3)</u>

Panama City Beach Series

Sun-Kissed Secrets (Book 1)
Sun-Kissed Secrets (Book 2)
Sun-Kissed Secrets (Book 3)

The Tainted Love Saga

Of Love and Deception (Book 1)
Of Love and Family (Book 2)
Of Love and Violence (Book 3)

Of Love and Abuse(Book 4)
Of Love and Crime (Book 5)
Of Love and Addiction (Book 6)
Of Love and Redemption (Book 7)

<u>Standalones</u>

Maiden's Blush

<u>Poetry</u>

Phantom Poetry
Lost and Found

Chapter One

The worn tires of Bella's rental car crunched over the gravel driveway as she pulled up to her childhood home, a quaint two-story farmhouse nestled among snow-dusted pine trees. She stepped out into the crisp December air, breathing in the familiar scent of wood smoke and cinnamon that always seemed to linger here during the holidays.

"There's my baby girl!" Lorena exclaimed, rushing out the front door and enveloping Bella in a warm hug before she could even grab her suitcase from the trunk. "Oh, let me look at you. Still as beautiful as ever. A little too thin though—have you been eating?"

Bella laughed, returning her mom's embrace. "Yes Mama, I eat."

"Well, we'll fix that. I've got a big pot of chicken and dumplings on the stove and an apple pie in the oven, just for you." Lorena stepped back, her eyes sparkling with joy and a hint of tears at having her daughter home.

As they entered the cozy living room, decorated with handmade quilts and family photos, Bella was nearly knocked over by an excited hug from her younger sister Chloe. "Bells! I can't believe you're really here! How long are you staying? There's so much to catch you up on. Did Mom tell you I'm engaged? Oh, and you'll never guess who else is back in town..."

Chloe's chatter faded into the background as Bella glanced around, soaking in the comforting familiarity of home. The well-worn armchair where Dad always sat to read the paper. Mom's collection of angel figurines on the mantel. The dent in the doorframe from when she and Chloe crashed their sled into it as kids.

She felt the tension of the city slowly melting from her shoulders. Maybe an unplanned Christmas trip home was exactly what she needed.

Settling into her old bedroom, Bella unpacked

her suitcase and hung up her clothes in the closet. She paused, running her fingers over the faded letterman jacket Hugh Blake—her old high school flame—had given her senior year. The soft wool brought back a flood of memories—football games, bonfires, stolen conversations under the bleachers. Bella sighed. She'd left that simple life behind long ago in pursuit of her big city dreams. But being back, surrounded by the warmth of her family and the memories of her youth, she couldn't help but wonder...had she made the right choice?

Bella shook her head, pushing aside the nostalgic thoughts. She had a successful career and a life in New York now. Still, something felt like it was missing, an emptiness in her heart that even orchestrating the most glamorous events couldn't fill.

Wandering over to the window, Bella gazed out at the snow-covered fields stretching toward the distant tree line. The peaceful winter landscape sparkled in the late afternoon sunlight. Smoke curled from the chimney of the Martins' farmhouse down the road. Bella smiled softly, remembering how she and Lacey Martin used to sled down that big hill, shrieking with laughter as they tumbled into piles of powdery snow.

She glanced upward, noticing a bright red

cardinal perched on a bare tree branch, a splash of vibrant color against the white and gray. Bella closed her eyes for a moment and whispered a quick prayer, as she used to do so often as a young girl in this very room.

"Lord, thank you for bringing me safely home to my family. I know I've been so caught up in work and neglected my faith lately. Please guide my steps while I'm here and help me find the purpose and fulfillment I've been missing. Quiet my anxious thoughts and fill me with Your perfect peace. In Jesus' name, amen."

Opening her eyes, Bella felt a renewed sense of clarity and calm wash over her. God had a plan. She just needed to trust in His timing. With a contented sigh, she headed downstairs to join her family, ready to embrace this unexpected season of coming home.

Chapter Two

The next morning, Bella woke to the aroma of fresh coffee and sizzling bacon. She padded downstairs in her fuzzy slippers, following the enticing scents to the kitchen where Lorena was bustling about, humming a cheerful tune.

"Good morning, sleepyhead," Lorena greeted her with a smile, setting a steaming mug of coffee in front of Bella as she slid onto a stool at the kitchen island. "I was just about to come wake you. Your father's out chopping wood for the fireplace, and Chloe ran to the store for some last-minute ingredients."

Bella wrapped her hands around the warm mug, inhaling the rich aroma. "Thanks, Mama. It feels so good to wake up here, without an alarm or a packed schedule waiting for me."

Lorena's eyes softened as she looked at her daughter. "You work too hard, baby girl. I'm glad you're taking some time for yourself. You know, sometimes the things we think we want in life aren't what truly matters in the end."

Before Bella could respond, the backdoor swung open with a gust of cold air, and in walked Hugh Blake, his arms loaded with firewood. Bella's heart stumbled in her chest at the sight of him, his cheeks ruddy from the cold and his blue eyes sparkling as they met hers.

"Well, look what the cat dragged in," Hugh drawled, a slow grin spreading across his face. "If it isn't Bella York, big city hotshot. Welcome home, darlin'."

Bella fought back a blush, hoping he couldn't hear the sudden pounding of her heart. "Hi, Hugh. It's been a while."

"Too long, if you ask me." He set the firewood down by the hearth, dusting off his hands. "I hear you're going to be helping with the festival. It'll be nice to have your expert touch. Lord knows we could use it."

Lorena clapped her hands together. "Oh, how

wonderful! It'll be just like old times, the two of you working together. Why don't you show Bella around town later, Hugh? Let her see how things have changed...and how they've stayed the same."

Bella shot her mother a look, but Lorena simply smiled innocently, a knowing twinkle in her eye.

"It would be my pleasure," Hugh said, his gaze never leaving Bella's. "I've got a few things to take care of at the station, but I'll swing by later to pick you up. We can grab lunch at Mabel's Diner, just like we used to."

As Hugh left, promising to return in a few hours, Bella sagged against the counter, her mind reeling. What was she getting herself into? She came home to escape the stress of work, not to dive head-first into the past she'd left behind.

But as she looked around the warm, inviting kitchen, memories of happier times flooding back, Bella couldn't help but feel a spark of excitement amid the nerves. Maybe there was a reason fate had brought her back to Pine Ridge this Christmas.

She finished her coffee and headed upstairs to get ready, determined to make the most of her time at home, even if that meant confronting the ghosts of her past—and the unresolved feelings she still carried for a certain handsome firefighter.

An hour later, Bella stood in front of the mirror, smoothing down her soft green sweater and fluffing her hair. She had to remind herself this wasn't a date, just two old friends catching up. No need to get worked up over Hugh Blake and his heart-stopping smile.

The doorbell rang and Bella's pulse leapt into double-time. She grabbed her coat and scarf, calling out a quick goodbye to her mom before stepping out into the chilly afternoon.

Hugh stood on the porch, looking far too good in a worn leather jacket and jeans. He grinned as Bella emerged, his eyes crinkling at the corners. "Wow, you look beautiful."

Bella ducked her head, hoping the cold would excuse the flush in her cheeks. "Flatterer. Let's get going before all the gossips in town see us and start planning our wedding."

Hugh chuckled, opening the passenger door of his pickup truck for her. "Would that be so bad? If I recall, half of them already had us hitched after the Harvest Dance senior year."

The memory brought a smile to Bella's lips as she climbed in, the scent of pine and Hugh's cologne enveloping her. That magical night seemed like a lifetime ago, when the future stretched out before them, full of possibilities.

As Hugh navigated the familiar streets, pointing out a few new shops and developments, Bella found herself relaxing, slipping back into the easy camaraderie they'd always shared. Maybe coming home for Christmas hadn't been such a crazy idea after all.

They pulled up to Mabel's Diner, the jukebox playing a country Christmas tune as they stepped inside the cozy restaurant. The owner herself, a stout woman in her 60s, let out a happy cry when she spotted them.

"Well, if it isn't little Bella York, back in town and prettier than a peach pie! Get on over here and give Mabel a hug!"

Bella obliged, breathing in the comforting scent of fried chicken and vanilla as Mabel's ample arms engulfed her. For the first time in ages, she felt herself truly exhale, the worries and pressures of her New York life fading like the steam from a cup of Mabel's chicory coffee.

As she and Hugh settled into a booth by the window, swapping stories and laughing over old memories, Bella marveled at how natural it felt to be here with him, like no time had passed at all. Mabel brought over two steaming plates of her famous meatloaf and mashed potatoes, giving them a wink.

Hugh's blue eyes sparkled with excitement as he suddenly exclaimed, "Hey, I almost forgot! The town's Christmas Eve festival is coming up, and we're a bit behind schedule. I know it's short notice, but we could really use your event planning expertise. What do you say?"

Bella hesitated, her mind already whirring with the logistics and challenges of pulling off a successful event on such a tight timeline. "I don't know, Hugh. It's been a while since I've done anything like this, especially in Pine Ridge."

"Come on, Bella," Hugh urged, his voice warm and encouraging. "It'll be just like old times. Remember how we used to plan the high school fundraisers together?"

A smile tugged at the corners of Bella's lips as memories of late-night brainstorming sessions and laughter-filled meetings flooded her mind. "Those were some pretty epic events," she acknowledged.

Hugh grinned, leaning closer to her. "Exactly. And with you on board, this festival will be the best one yet. Plus, it'll give us a chance to spend more time together."

Bella's heart skipped a beat at the prospect of

working alongside Hugh, but a flicker of doubt crept in. Was she ready to dive headfirst into small-town life again, even if only for a short while?

She glanced around at the quaint diner and friendly faces, a wave of nostalgia washing over her. Perhaps this was exactly what she needed—a chance to reconnect with her roots and rediscover the joy she'd left behind in the pursuit of her career.

Taking a deep breath, Bella met Hugh's hopeful gaze. "Alright, I'm in. Let's make this the most unforgettable Christmas Eve festival Pine Ridge has ever seen."

Hugh's face lit up with a dazzling smile as he dug into his food.

Bella picked up her fork and as she took a bite, she couldn't help but wonder if agreeing to help with the festival would lead to more than just event planning. With Hugh by her side and the magic of the holidays in the air, anything seemed possible.

Chapter Three

Bella stepped into the cozy Pine Ridge Coffee Shop, a cheerful bell tinkling above the door. The warm scent of fresh-brewed coffee and buttery pastries enveloped her as she glanced around the room. A group of people gathered at a large table in the corner, and her heart skipped a beat when she spotted Hugh at the head of it, his broad shoulders filling out a blue flannel shirt.

"Bella, over here!" Hugh called out, waving her over with a dazzling smile.

She made her way to the table, shaking hands and greeting the other committee members. "Thanks for having me," she said brightly, taking a seat across from Hugh. "I'm excited to help out however I can."

As the meeting got underway, Bella was

impressed by Hugh's passion and dedication to the festival. He had a clear vision and dozens of ideas, from a gingerbread house contest to a nostalgic hayride. His blue eyes sparkled as he spoke animatedly.

He really cares about this town and keeping traditions alive, Bella thought, finding herself smiling at his enthusiasm. *It's nice to see him putting his all into something so wholesome.*

Before long, Bella found herself chiming in, unable to resist sharing some of her professional insights. "In my experience, a signature color scheme and cohesive branding across all the events can really elevate a festival," she suggested. "Maybe we could work in some pine green and silver, give everything a magical winter wonderland vibe."

Hugh's brow furrowed. "I don't know, I kind of like the homespun charm of how we've always done it," he countered. "Handmade signage, classic red and green. It is a Christmas festival after all."

"Yes, but with a few modern touches, we could attract visitors from all the surrounding towns, make it a real destination event," Bella pushed back gently.

As they debated back and forth, trading ideas, Bella felt an undeniable spark of attraction alongside the tension. There was just something about the passion in Hugh's eyes and the timbre of his Southern drawl that made her pulse quicken. He met her gaze and held it a beat too long, a playful challenge in his expression.

Get it together, Bella, she scolded herself. *You're here to help your hometown, not fall for your high school sweetheart all over again.*

Still, as the meeting wrapped up, she couldn't deny the warmth that spread through her chest as Hugh turned that knee-weakening smile on her once more. "I'm really glad you're a part of this, Bella. You're going to be a huge help."

Gathering her things, Bella returned the smile, trying to ignore the giddy flutter in her stomach. "I'm happy to do it. Guess we'll have to learn to compromise, huh?"

"Guess so," Hugh agreed with a chuckle. "I'm looking forward to it."

As Bella headed out into the crisp December air, she knew one thing for certain—this festival was going to be full of surprises. And maybe, just maybe, a chance to reconnect with the man she'd never quite been able to forget.

The aroma of freshly brewed coffee enveloped Bella as she settled into a cozy booth at the local diner. Across from her, Hugh slid into his seat, his blue eyes crinkling at the corners as he smiled. "I'm really glad we could catch up like this," he said, his voice warm and familiar.

Bella wrapped her hands around her steaming mug, savoring the heat against her palms. "Me too," she admitted. "It's been a long time." She paused, memories of their shared past flickering through her mind. "Do you ever think about... about what might have been?"

Hugh's gaze turned thoughtful, his smile tinged with a hint of melancholy. "Sometimes," he confessed. "I wonder if things would have been different if we'd tried harder to make it work."

Bella nodded, a lump forming in her throat. "We were so young then," she mused. "And I was so focused on my career. I didn't know how to balance it all."

Hugh reached across the table, his hand briefly covering hers in a comforting gesture. "We both had a lot of growing up to do," he said gently. "But look at us now—we've come a long way."

As they sipped their coffee and reminisced about old times, Bella couldn't help but notice the way

Hugh's gaze lingered on her, the unspoken emotions swirling between them. Despite the years apart, the connection they'd once shared seemed to shimmer just beneath the surface, waiting to be rekindled.

But as much as her heart yearned to explore those feelings, Bella knew she had to tread carefully. Her life in New York, her thriving career—they weren't things she could just walk away from on a whim. And Hugh... he was the embodiment of everything she'd left behind. The comfort, the familiarity, the slower pace of small-town life that both called to her and made her hesitate.

"So, tell me more about your work in the city," Hugh prompted, his voice cutting through her thoughts. "It sounds like you've really made a name for yourself."

Bella smiled, grateful for the change of subject. "It's been a wild ride," she acknowledged. "I've had the opportunity to plan some incredible events. Galas, product launches, even a few celebrity weddings."

Hugh let out a low whistle. "Color me impressed. Sounds like you're living the dream."

But was she? The question hung unspoken in the air between them. Bella shifted in her seat, suddenly feeling the weight of her exhaustion, the toll of countless late nights and high-pressure deadlines. "It's rewarding," she said carefully. "But sometimes I wonder if it's all worth it. If I'm missing out on the things that really matter."

Hugh's expression softened, understanding etched in the lines of his face. "You know, Bella, it's never too late to make a change. To come home."

Home. The word seemed to echo in her chest, a siren song she couldn't quite ignore. But before she could respond, the jingle of the bell above the diner door shattered the moment. Bella glanced up to see a group of Hugh's fellow firefighters trooping in, their laughter and boisterous chatter filling the space.

"Duty calls," Hugh said with a rueful grin, sliding out of the booth. "But think about what I said, okay? Pine Ridge will always be here for you. And so will I."

With a final squeeze of her hand, he was gone, leaving Bella alone with her thoughts and the cooling dregs of her coffee. She watched him go, marveling at the easy way he greeted his friends, the camaraderie and sense of purpose that seemed to radiate from him. It was a far cry from the cutthroat world of corporate event planning, where every smile was calculated and every relationship a means to an end.

Maybe Hugh was right. Maybe it was time to

reevaluate her priorities, to figure out what truly made her happy. But as Bella gathered her things and stepped out into the brisk winter air, she knew one thing for certain—the decision wouldn't be an easy one. With the festival looming and her heart pulled in two different directions, she had a feeling the coming weeks would be full of surprises, both professional and personal.

Taking a deep breath, Bella squared her shoulders and headed down the quaint, decorated street. There was work to be done, and she was determined to make this festival the best one the town had seen yet.

Chapter Four

In the days that followed, Bella threw herself into planning the festival, determined to make it a success. She spent long hours organizing vendors for the winter market, coordinating with local businesses, and fine-tuning the details of the tree lighting ceremony.

As she stood in the town square, watching the bustling activity around her, Bella felt a sense of pride and belonging that she hadn't experienced in years. The twinkling lights, the laughter of children, the scent of pine and cinnamon in the air—it all reminded her of the magic of her hometown.

Hugh appeared at her side, his presence comforting and familiar. "It's really coming together," he remarked, surveying the scene with an appreciative eye. "You've done an amazing job, Bella."

Bella turned to him, a smile playing on her lips. "I couldn't have done it without you," she said sincerely. "Your support has meant everything to me."

As they stood together, watching the festival come to life around them, Bella realized that her heart felt fuller than it had in a long time. The joy of contributing to her community, of reconnecting with old friends and cherished memories, filled her with a warmth that even the chilly December air couldn't diminish.

And as Hugh's hand brushed against hers, sending a tingle up her arm, Bella couldn't help but wonder if maybe, just maybe, she'd found something even more precious than success—a chance to rediscover the love she'd once left behind.

Bella tossed and turned in her childhood bed, the moonlight casting a soft glow through the lace curtains. Her mind raced with thoughts of Hugh, their conversation from earlier playing on repeat. She couldn't shake the feeling of warmth that had spread through her when he'd smiled at her, the way his eyes had sparkled with genuine affection.

Bella sighed, flipping onto her back and staring up at the familiar ceiling. The same glow-in-the-dark stars she'd stuck there as a teenager winked back at her, a remnant of a simpler time. A time when her biggest worry was whether Hugh would ask her to the homecoming dance, not juggling the demands of a high-powered career and the growing ache in her heart for the life she'd left behind.

She thought back to their years together, the easy laughter and stolen kisses, the way they'd dreamed of a future side by side. But then college had called, and the bright lights of the city had beckoned. She'd been so sure of her path, so determined to make a name for herself. And she had—but at what cost?

Bella's phone buzzed on the nightstand, jolting her from her reverie. She reached for it, squinting at the bright screen. A text from her assistant, reminding her of a conference call scheduled for first thing in the morning. Bella groaned, the weight of her responsibilities crashing back down on her shoulders.

But as she set the phone aside and burrowed back under the covers, Bella's thoughts drifted once again to Hugh. To the way he'd looked at her across the table, the unspoken promise in his eyes. The festival was just the beginning, she realized. A chance to reconnect, to explore the possibility of a future that looked very different from the one she'd always imagined.

She sighed, sitting up and hugging her knees to her chest. The silence of the house was broken only by the gentle ticking of the clock on her nightstand. Bella glanced at the framed photos lining her dresser—snapshots of her life in New York, the glittering events she'd orchestrated, the accolades she'd received. But none of them filled her with the same sense of contentment as the simple joys of Pine Ridge—and Hugh.

A soft knock at the door startled her from her reverie. "Bella, honey? Are you awake?" Lorena's voice was gentle, laced with maternal concern.

"Come in, Mom," Bella called, smoothing her tangled hair.

Lorena entered, wrapped in a cozy robe, and perched on the edge of the bed. "Can't sleep?" she asked, her eyes filled with understanding.

Bella shook her head. "I just...I can't stop thinking about everything. The festival, being back home...Hugh."

"Oh, sweetheart," Lorena murmured, pulling

Bella into a hug. "It's okay to feel conflicted. Your life in New York, it's everything you've worked for. But your heart, it remembers what it's like to be here, to be with the people who love you."

Bella leaned into her mother's embrace, tears pricking at the corners of her eyes. "I don't know what to do, Mom. I love my job, but being here...it feels right. And Hugh...Truth be told, I never stopped caring about him."

Lorena stroked Bella's hair, a knowing smile on her face. "Sometimes, the heart knows what it wants, even when the mind is unsure. Don't be afraid to listen to it, Bella. You might be surprised where it leads you."

As her mother's words washed over her, Bella felt a glimmer of clarity amidst the confusion. Maybe, just maybe, she could find a way to balance her dreams with the tug of her hometown—and the love she'd never quite let go of.

Chapter Five

Bella balanced precariously on the ladder, stretching to loop a strand of twinkling lights around the towering Christmas tree in the center of the town square. The crisp December air nipped at her nose as she focused on her task, determined to make the tree look perfect.

"Hey there, need a hand?" Hugh called out, approaching with a friendly grin. He wore a thick flannel jacket that accentuated his broad shoulders.

Bella glanced down, momentarily distracted by the way his blue eyes sparkled in the late afternoon sun. "I've got it under control, thanks," she replied, reaching for another strand of lights.

Hugh chuckled, shaking his head. "Come on,

Bells. You know I'm taller than you. Let me help." He held out his hand expectantly.

With an exaggerated sigh, Bella passed him the lights. "Fine, but I'm in charge of the overall design."

"Yes, ma'am," Hugh teased, easily reaching the higher branches. They worked together in comfortable silence for a few minutes, the only sounds the rustling of pine needles and the distant chatter of other volunteers setting up booths.

As Bella stepped back to admire their handiwork, she felt a sudden rush of nostalgia. How many times had she and Hugh decorated this very tree as teenagers, laughing and sneaking sips of hot chocolate? The memories warmed her from the inside out.

"Looks good," Hugh said, interrupting her thoughts. "But I think we need more red ornaments to balance it out."

Bella raised an eyebrow. "Oh, do you? And when did you become such a decoration expert?"

Hugh grinned, unphased by her teasing. "I've always had an eye for design. Remember when I helped you decorate the gym for the winter formal junior year?"

"You mean when you almost set the streamers on fire with those cheap Christmas lights?" Bella countered, unable to hide her smile.

"Hey, it added ambiance," Hugh argued, his eyes twinkling with mirth.

They dissolved into laughter, the sound carrying across the square. Bella felt a sudden pang in her chest. She had missed this easy banter more than she realized.

Before she could dwell on it further, a familiar voice called out, "Well, well, if it isn't Bella York, back in the flesh!"

Bella turned to see her childhood best friend, Melanie, approaching with a wide grin. "Mel!" she exclaimed, pulling the other woman into a tight hug. "It's so good to see you."

Mel squeezed her back before holding her at arm's length, appraising her. "Look at you, Miss Fancy New York City Event Planner. I can't believe you managed to tear yourself away from the big city for little old Pine Ridge."

Bella rolled her eyes good-naturedly. "Oh you know, I could never miss the Christmas festival."

Mel's gaze slid over to Hugh, who was busying himself with untangling a strand of lights. "And I'm sure a certain firefighter had nothing to do with your decision to come back, right?"

Bella felt her cheeks warm, and she swatted at Mel's arm. "Stop it. Hugh and I are just friends."

"Uh-huh," Mel said, unconvinced. "Friends who used to be joined at the hip every Christmas. I seem to remember a certain mistletoe incident at the festival a few years back..."

"That was a long time ago," Bella interrupted, her face now fully flushed. She glanced at Hugh, but he seemed not to have heard, too focused on his task.

Mel held up her hands in mock surrender. "Okay, okay. I'm just saying, it's nice to see you two together again. It feels like old times."

Bella's heart squeezed at the thought. She had spent so long trying to move forward, to build a new life for herself in New York. But being back in Pine Ridge, surrounded by the warmth of her old friends and the twinkling lights of the town square, she couldn't help but wonder if she had left a piece of herself behind.

As if sensing her thoughts, Hugh looked up and caught her eye, his smile soft and familiar. Bella smiled back, feeling a flicker of something she couldn't quite name. Maybe Mel was right. Maybe there was still a chance for old times, after all.

Chapter Six

Bella wandered through the quiet streets of Pine Ridge, her mind awash with memories of Christmases past. The crisp evening air carried the scent of chimney smoke and pine, transporting her back to her teenage years.

The stars twinkled overhead as Bella walked along the quiet streets of Pine Ridge, her footsteps echoing in the stillness of the night. She pulled her coat tighter around her, the chill of the winter air a welcome respite from the warmth of the fire and the intensity of Hugh's gaze.

She couldn't shake the feeling of his presence, the way he had looked at her as if he could see straight into her soul. It was a look that spoke of a history, of moments shared and feelings left unspoken. Bella sighed, her breath forming a misty cloud in the air.

The town square came into view, the Christmas lights twinkling merrily in the darkness. Bella paused, taking in the sight of the massive tree at the center, its branches heavy with ornaments and tinsel. It was a sight that had always filled her with joy, but tonight, it only served to remind her of how much had changed.

She thought of New York, of the life she had built there. The high-profile events, the glitz and glamour, the sense of accomplishment that came with each successful project. But as she stood there, surrounded by the quiet beauty of her hometown, Bella couldn't help but wonder if that was truly what she wanted.

Her mind drifted to Hugh, to the way he made her feel. With him, she wasn't just Bella York, the high-powered event planner. She was simply Bella, the girl who had grown up with dreams of a different life. The girl who had once believed in the magic of Christmas and the power of love.

Bella closed her eyes, letting the memories wash over her. The snowball fights, the hot chocolate by the fire, the stolen kisses under the mistletoe. It all seemed so long ago, but standing there, in the heart of Pine Ridge, it felt as if no time had passed at all.

She opened her eyes, her gaze settling on the church at the edge of the square. The same church where she and Hugh had once made a promise, a promise to always be there for each other. Bella felt a tug at her heart, a longing for something she couldn't quite name.

She kept walking and then paused in front of the old cinema, its marquee now dark, remembering the countless holiday movies she and Hugh had watched together, huddled close in the worn velvet seats.

A soft smile played on her lips as she recalled the way Hugh would always insist on buying her favorite candy, how their hands would brush as they reached for the popcorn. Those small moments had meant everything to her then, and even now, they stirred a warmth in her chest.

Lost in thought, Bella barely noticed the crunch of footsteps behind her until a familiar voice called out, "Penny for your thoughts?"

She turned to find Hugh approaching, a box of festival decorations tucked under his arm. "Oh, just taking a little trip down memory lane," she replied, tucking a strand of hair behind her ear.

"This old place does bring back a lot of memories," Hugh said, nodding toward the cinema. "Remember when we convinced the projectionist to let us stay past closing to watch 'It's a Wonderful Life'?"

Bella laughed. "How could I forget? We ended up falling asleep and nearly gave our parents a heart attack when they couldn't find us."

They fell into a comfortable silence, the weight of their shared history hanging between them. Hugh shifted the box in his arms. "I was just heading over to your place to drop these off. Mind if I walk with you?"

"Not at all," Bella said, falling into step beside him.

As they approached her house, Bella couldn't help but feel a flutter of nerves. Being around Hugh again, it was all too easy to slip back into old patterns, old feelings. She unlocked the door and led him inside, the warmth of the fireplace enveloping them as they entered the living room.

Hugh set the box down and straightened up, his gaze meeting hers. In the soft light, his blue eyes seemed to dance with unspoken emotion. Bella's breath caught in her throat, a thousand words rising to her lips, only to fade away unspoken.

They stood there for a moment, the crackle of

the fire the only sound in the room. Hugh took a step closer, his hand lifting as if to touch her cheek, but he hesitated. "Bella, I..."

But the words wouldn't come. He let his hand fall back to his side, a rueful smile on his face. "I should probably get going. Early day tomorrow."

Bella nodded, not trusting herself to speak. She walked him to the door, her heart heavy with all the things left unsaid. As Hugh stepped out into the night, he paused, turning back to look at her. "Goodnight, Bella."

"Goodnight, Hugh," she whispered, watching as he disappeared into the darkness.

She closed the door and leaned against it, closing her eyes. The past and the present had collided tonight, leaving her more uncertain than ever about her future. But one thing was clear: her feelings for Hugh, buried though they had been, were far from gone.

With a sigh, Bella pushed off from the door and headed for the stairs. Tomorrow was a new day, and perhaps, with a little Christmas magic, it would bring the clarity she so desperately needed.

Chapter Seven

Bella's heart sank as she caught sight of Hugh and Rachel through the fogged window of the diner. Rachel Winters, Hugh's ex-girlfriend. Last she'd heard, Rachel had left Pine Ridge to live in Nashville and pursue her country music dreams. Rachel was the woman Hugh had turned to after Bella had left for New York, leaving behind a trail of broken promises and unspoken feelings.

Rachel looked as stunning as ever, with her golden curls cascading down her back and her bright blue eyes sparkling with laughter. She leaned closer to Hugh, placing a perfectly manicured hand on his arm as she spoke animatedly. Hugh, ever the gentleman, smiled politely, but Bella couldn't help but notice the way his eyes crinkled at the corners—a telltale sign of his genuine amusement.

As Bella watched the scene unfold, memories of her past with Hugh flooded her mind. The late-night talks under the stars, the stolen glances across crowded rooms, and the almost-kisses that never quite happened. She had always believed that their love story was unfinished, that fate would somehow bring them back together. But seeing him with Rachel now, so at ease and comfortable, made her wonder if she had missed her chance.

The diner's neon sign cast a soft glow on the sidewalk, illuminating the falling snowflakes that danced in the chilly evening air. The scent of freshly baked apple pie wafted from the kitchen, mingling with the aroma of coffee and the faint trace of Hugh's cologne that lingered in Bella's memory. She pulled her coat tighter around her, suddenly feeling the weight of her loneliness pressing down on her chest.

Hugh and Rachel's heads were bowed close together, a familiarity in their posture that made her stomach twist. She watched as Hugh leaned back, laughing at something Rachel said, a fond look on his face.

The bell above the door jingled as Bella entered,

catching Hugh's attention. His smile faltered briefly as he registered Bella's presence.

"Bella, hey," he said, rising to greet her. "You remember Rachel?"

Rachel turned, flashing a perfect white smile. "Bella, so good to see you again! It's been too long."

"Rachel. I didn't know you were back in town." Bella tried to keep her tone light, but she couldn't help the hint of accusation that crept in.

"Just for the holidays," Rachel said breezily. "Thought I'd surprise this one." She nudged Hugh playfully.

Hugh rubbed the back of his neck, looking sheepish. "Yeah, it was definitely a surprise. We were just catching up."

"I can see that," Bella said coolly. An awkward silence fell over the table.

"Well, I should get going," Rachel said finally, standing to leave. "It was great seeing you both." She gave Hugh a lingering hug before sashaying out the door, leaving a cloud of expensive perfume in her wake.

Bella slid into the booth across from Hugh, studying the menu intently to avoid his gaze. Her mind raced with questions she was afraid to ask.

Hugh cleared his throat, breaking the silence. "So, how are the festival plans coming along?"

Bella looked up from the menu, meeting his eyes. "Fine," she said shortly. "The committee is making good progress."

"That's great." Hugh fidgeted with his coffee mug. "Listen, Bella, about Rachel—"

"You don't owe me an explanation," Bella interrupted, her tone sharper than she intended. "It's none of my business."

Hugh frowned. "I just want you to know that—"

But then, the waitress arrived to take their order, breaking the charged moment between them. Which was probably for the best because after she left, Bella quickly steered the conversation to menial small talk about the festival and life in Pine Ridge.

Hugh easily followed her leave, and Bella felt the tension leave her shoulders.

While part of her was dying to know what Hugh was going to say, the other part of her was relieved to not know, in case it was something she wasn't ready to hear.

Probably for the best...

Chapter Eight

At the next festival planning meeting, Bella found it hard to concentrate. She shuffled papers and tapped her pen restlessly as Hugh gave his updates, his voice washing over her without registering.

"Bella? Thoughts on the lighting setup?" Mayor Thompson's voice snapped her out of her reverie.

"What? Oh, um, I think we should stick with the plan from last year. It worked well." She avoided Hugh's questioning look.

As the meeting wrapped up, Hugh approached her. "Everything okay? You seemed a little distracted."

Bella busied herself with packing up her bag.

"I'm fine, just a lot on my mind with the festival planning."

"You sure? You know you can talk to me about anything." Hugh's blue eyes were filled with concern.

"I'm sure," Bella said briskly. "I should get going. I have a lot of work to do."

"Wait, I thought maybe we could grab dinner, talk through some of the details-"

"I can't tonight. Rain check?" Bella shouldered her bag and headed for the door, leaving Hugh standing alone, a puzzled frown on his face.

As she walked to her car, Bella mentally kicked herself. What was she doing, pushing Hugh away like this? But the image of him and Rachel, heads bent together, kept playing in her mind. She needed to get her head on straight before she said something she'd regret.

The next morning dawned crisp and clear. Bella arrived early to oversee the setup, her mind still preoccupied with thoughts of Hugh and Rachel. She busied herself with checking off tasks, barely registering the tangle of lights and garlands transforming the town square.

When Hugh arrived with the rest of the fire department to hang the lights, Bella felt her heart lurch. His presence was like a live wire sparking through the air. But as he approached, she turned away, pretending to be engrossed in her clipboard.

"Morning," he said, his tone even.

"Morning," she replied, eyes still fixed on her list. "The lights need to go up on the gazebo first."

"Got it." Hugh hesitated, clearly wanting to say more, but Bella was already moving on to the next task.

As the day wore on, their interactions remained strained and distant. The easy banter and inside jokes that normally flowed between them were replaced by stilted sentences and fleeting glances. Bella could sense Hugh's confusion and concern, but she didn't know how to explain the tangle of jealousy and fear knotting in her chest.

By the time dusk fell, exhaustion and emotion had taken their toll. As the mayor droned on in the mic doing sound check, Bella snuck out and slumped onto a bench in the park, head in her hands. Tears pricked behind her eyes, but she blinked them back.

Snow was falling softly, frosting her hair and shoulders, when the bench creaked beside her. Without looking up, she knew it was Hugh.

"Bella." His voice was gentle. "What's going on with you? You've been avoiding me all day."

She took a shuddering breath, trying to find the right words. "You and Rachel the other day. At the diner. You looked...close."

Hugh was quiet for a moment. Then... "Rachel and I dated a long time ago. A lifetime ago. When she showed up, it brought back a lot of memories. But that's all they are, memories."

Bella looked up at him then, seeing the earnest sincerity in his eyes. "I thought...I don't know what I thought."

"You thought I still had feelings for her?" His mouth quirked into a rueful smile.

Bella felt foolish suddenly. She shrugged helplessly.

But then, other members of the committee came up, breaking up their conversation.

Bella stepped back, grateful for the break in their conversation. She was relieved and confused all at once. True, she didn't want to see him with Rachel, but she also wasn't entirely sure what she wanted either. Her head was just such a mess.

As she walked through the snowy streets of Pine Ridge, Bella's thoughts drifted to her sister, Chloe. She had always been Bella's confidante and voice of reason. Pulling out her phone, Bella dialed Chloe's number, hoping she would pick up.

"Hey, sis! How's the festival planning going?" Chloe's warm voice filled Bella's ear.

"It's...complicated," Bella sighed. "I need your advice."

"I'm all ears. What's going on?"

Bella found a quiet bench near the town square and sat down, brushing away the snow. She took a deep breath and began to explain her situation with Hugh, the jealousy she felt seeing him with Rachel, and the argument they'd just had.

Chloe listened patiently, humming in understanding. "It sounds like you're afraid of getting hurt again, Bella. But from what you've told me about Hugh, he seems like a genuine guy who really cares about you."

"He is," Bella admitted, watching her breath form tiny clouds in the cold air. "But what if I'm just setting myself up for heartbreak?"

"You can't live your life in fear of what might happen," Chloe said gently. "Sometimes, you have to take a leap of faith and trust in the goodness of others. And in yourself."

Bella let her sister's words sink in. She knew Chloe was right. Running away from her feelings for Hugh would only lead to regret.

"I think it's time you give Pine Ridge—and

Hugh—a real chance," Chloe continued. "You've been so focused on your career in New York, but maybe what you've been searching for has been right in front of you all along."

Tears pricked at the corners of Bella's eyes. "Thank you, sis. I don't know what I'd do without you."

"That's what I'm here for," Chloe said warmly. "Best sister ever."

"Yes, you are," Bella agreed.

Chapter Nine

Golden sunlight streamed through the lace curtains, gently rousing Bella from her slumber. She stretched, feeling the warm quilted comforter slide off her shoulders. Today was a new day, a chance for a fresh start.

Bella sat up, determination etched on her face. No more distractions, no more confusion about Hugh. The Christmas festival needed her full attention.

After a quick shower, Bella slipped into her favorite jeans and a cozy red sweater. She grabbed her notebook, already brimming with ideas, and headed out the door. The crisp December air nipped at her cheeks as she walked briskly towards the town hall, her boots crunching on the frosty sidewalk.

Inside, Bella found the festival committee already assembled, chatting excitedly over steaming mugs of coffee. She smiled, feeding off their energy. "Good morning, everyone! Let's dive right in, shall we?"

For the next hour, Bella immersed herself in planning, her pen flying across the pages as she jotted down ideas and delegated tasks. The townspeople watched in awe, impressed by her efficiency and creativity. Bella glowed with pride, thrilled to be making a difference in her hometown.

As the meeting wrapped up, Bella gathered her notes, ready to tackle the next item on her list. She turned, nearly colliding with a solid chest. Hugh. Her heart stuttered as she met his blue eyes, still as captivating as ever.

"Bella, hi," Hugh said softly, his deep voice sending shivers down her spine. "You're doing an amazing job with the festival."

"Thanks, Hugh," Bella replied, trying to keep her tone light. "Just doing my part."

They stared at each other for a long moment, the air thick with unspoken words. Bella's mind raced, questions and emotions swirling inside her. But she couldn't go there, not now. She had a job to do.

"Well, I should get going," Bella said, breaking the silence. "Lots to do before the festival."

Hugh nodded, a flicker of disappointment in his eyes. "Of course. I'll see you around, Bella."

As Bella walked away, she could feel Hugh's gaze on her back, the weight of their history pressing down on her. But she pushed those thoughts aside, focusing instead on the task at hand. The festival needed her, and she wouldn't let anything, not even her own heart, get in the way.

The sun had just begun to set when Bella received an urgent call from the festival committee. "Bella, we have a problem," the voice on the other end said, panic evident in their tone. "The Christmas lights in the town square aren't working, and we can't seem to fix them. If we don't get them up and running, we might have to cancel the festival."

Bella's heart sank. She knew how much the festival meant to the town, and she couldn't bear the thought of letting everyone down. "I'm on my way," she said firmly, grabbing her coat and rushing out the door.

When she arrived at the town square, Bella found a small crowd gathered around the unlit Christmas tree, their faces etched with worry. She spotted Hugh among them, his brow furrowed as he examined the tangled strands of lights.

"What's the situation?" Bella asked, approaching Hugh.

He looked up, his eyes filled with determination. "It looks like a few of the bulbs are burnt out, and it's causing the whole strand to malfunction. We need to replace them, but we don't have any spares on hand."

Bella's mind raced, trying to think of a solution. Suddenly, an idea struck her. "What about the hardware store? They might have some in stock."

Hugh's face lit up. "That's a great idea, Bella. I'll head over there now and see what I can find."

As Hugh hurried off, Bella turned her attention to the crowd, offering reassuring words and promising to do everything in her power to fix the problem. She could feel the weight of their expectations on her shoulders, but she refused to let it crush her.

Minutes turned into hours as Bella and the festival committee worked tirelessly to untangle the lights and replace the faulty bulbs. The sun had long since set by the time they finished, but as Bella stood back to admire their handiwork, she couldn't help but feel a sense of pride.

The town square was now awash in a soft, warm

glow, the twinkling lights casting a magical spell over the scene. Bella felt a presence beside her and turned to find Hugh, a small smile playing at the corners of his mouth.

"You did it," he said softly, his eyes reflecting the glow of the lights.

Bella shook her head. "We did it. Together."

They stood in silence for a moment, surrounded by the twinkling lights and the distant chatter of the townspeople. Bella could feel the warmth of Hugh's body beside her, and she fought the urge to lean into him.

"Bella, I..." Hugh began, his voice low and hesitant. "I know things between us are complicated, but I just wanted to say..."

Bella's heart raced as she waited for him to continue, but the words seemed to catch in Hugh's throat. He looked down, his brow furrowed.

"I'm just really glad you're back," he finished quietly.

Bella swallowed, her own emotions threatening to overwhelm her. She wanted to tell him everything, to pour out her heart and confess the feelings she'd been holding onto for so long. But something held her back, a fear of vulnerability that she couldn't quite shake.

"Me too, Hugh," she said instead, her voice barely above a whisper. "Me too."

They stood there a moment longer, the unspoken words hanging in the air between them. Then, with a small smile, Hugh turned and walked away, leaving Bella alone with her thoughts and the twinkling lights of the town square.

Chapter Ten

Bella was just tidying up the last of the decorations in the town square when she heard a familiar voice calling her name. She turned to see her sister hurrying towards her, a wide grin on her face.

"Bella!" Chloe exclaimed, pulling her into a warm hug. "I've been looking all over for you. The town square looks absolutely magical, by the way. You've really outdone yourself."

Bella stepped back, taking in her sister's appearance. Chloe was dressed to the nines, her blonde hair swept up into an elegant updo and her lithe figure draped in a shimmering silver gown. "Thanks, Chlo," Bella said, smiling. "But what's with the fancy getup? You look like you're headed to a ball."

Chloe's eyes widened. "Don't tell me you forgot! The Winter Ball is tonight, and you promised you'd be there."

Bella's heart skipped a beat. The Winter Ball. Of course. How could she have let it slip her mind? She'd been so caught up in the festival preparations that she'd completely forgotten about the town's annual holiday soirée.

"Oh, Chlo, I'm so sorry," Bella said, her face falling. "I've just been so busy with the festival, and-"

"No excuses," Chloe interrupted, holding up a hand. "You're coming with me, and that's final. I've already picked out the perfect dress for you."

Bella hesitated, biting her lip. The thought of attending the ball sent a flutter of nerves through her stomach. It wasn't that she didn't want to go—in fact, the idea of dressing up and dancing the night away sounded like the perfect way to unwind after the stress of festival planning. But there was one thing holding her back, one question that she couldn't quite shake.

"Do you think...do you think Hugh will be there?" Bella asked, her voice barely above a whisper.

Chloe's eyes softened, and she reached out to squeeze Bella's hand. "I don't know, honey. But even if he is, you can't let that stop you from enjoying yourself. You deserve a night of fun and relaxation, and I won't take no for an answer."

Bella sighed, knowing her sister was right. She couldn't keep putting her life on hold because of her complicated history with Hugh. It was time to move forward, to embrace the present and all the possibilities it held.

"Alright, Chlo," Bella said, a small smile tugging at the corners of her mouth. "Let's do this."

An hour later, Bella found herself standing in front of the full-length mirror in her bedroom, hardly recognizing the woman staring back at her. The dress Chloe had chosen was a deep, rich emerald green, with a sweetheart neckline and a flowing skirt that swished around her ankles. Her hair was swept up into a loose chignon, with a few tendrils framing her face. She looked elegant, sophisticated, and entirely unlike her usual self.

"Wow," Chloe breathed, appearing behind Bella in the mirror. "You look stunning, sis. Hugh won't know what hit him."

Bella's heart fluttered at the mention of Hugh's name, but she quickly pushed the thought aside.

Tonight wasn't about him. It was about her, and the fresh start she was determined to make.

The Winter Ball was in full swing by the time Bella and Chloe arrived at the town's community center. The room was adorned with sparkling snowflakes and shimmering icicles, creating a magical winter wonderland. Soft music filled the air as couples swayed on the dance floor, their laughter and chatter mingling with the melodies.

Bella smoothed her hands over her emerald green dress, the silky fabric hugging her curves. She scanned the room, her heart fluttering with a mix of anticipation and nervousness. Would Hugh be here tonight? After their moment in the town square, she couldn't help but wonder if things might finally change between them.

As she made her way through the crowd, Bella was greeted by familiar faces, each expressing their gratitude for her help with the festival. She smiled and exchanged pleasantries, but her mind was elsewhere, constantly searching for a glimpse of Hugh.

Just as she was about to give up hope, a familiar voice caught her attention. "Bella, you look stunning."

She turned to find Hugh standing before her, dressed in a dashing suit that accentuated his broad shoulders and strong jawline. His blue eyes sparkled as he took in the sight of her, a soft smile playing on his lips.

"Hugh, you made it," Bella said, trying to keep her voice steady despite the quickening of her heartbeat. She took in his handsome appearance, the way his suit perfectly complemented his rugged features.

He stepped closer, his gaze never leaving hers. "I wouldn't miss it for the world. Especially not after everything you've done for this town, Bella. You're incredible."

A blush crept up Bella's cheeks at his praise. She looked down, suddenly feeling shy under the intensity of his gaze. "I was just doing my job, Hugh. Anyone would have done the same."

Hugh reached out and gently tilted her chin up, forcing her to meet his eyes once more. "No, not anyone. You're special, Bella. You always have been."

The sincerity in his voice made Bella's heart flutter. She opened her mouth to respond, but the words caught in her throat as the music shifted to a slow, romantic melody.

Hugh held out his hand, a silent invitation. "May I have this dance?"

Bella hesitated for only a moment before placing her hand in his. His fingers curled around hers, warm and strong, as he led her onto the dance floor. He pulled her close, one hand resting on the small of her back while the other held hers against his chest.

They swayed to the music, their bodies moving in perfect sync. Bella could feel the heat of Hugh's touch through the thin fabric of her dress, sending shivers down her spine. She rested her head on his shoulder, breathing in his familiar scent of pine and wood smoke.

For a few precious moments, the world around them faded away. There was no festival, no responsibilities, no unspoken feelings hanging in the air between them. There was only Hugh and Bella, two hearts beating as one.

As the song came to an end, Hugh pulled back slightly, his blue eyes searching Bella's face. She could see the unspoken questions in his gaze, the longing and the uncertainty.

"Bella," he whispered, his voice rough with emotion. "I know we have a lot to figure out, but I need you to know..."

He trailed off, his brow furrowing as he struggled to find the right words. Bella's heart raced, her breath catching in her throat as she waited for him to continue.

But before Hugh could speak, a commotion

from the entrance of the community center caught their attention. They turned to see a group of people rushing in, their faces etched with worry and fear.

"There's a fire at the old Miller farm!" someone shouted, their voice filled with panic. "We need help!"

Hugh's eyes widened, his body tensing as he shifted into firefighter mode. He turned to Bella, an apology written on his face.

"I'm sorry, Bella. I have to go."

Bella nodded, understanding the urgency of the situation. "Go. Do what you need to do. I'll be here when you get back."

With a final squeeze of her hand, Hugh rushed off, disappearing into the crowd as he made his way towards the exit. Bella watched him go, her heart heavy with worry and unspoken emotions.

She turned back to the dance floor, suddenly feeling lost and alone among the swirling couples. The magic of the moment had been shattered, replaced by a sense of unease and uncertainty.

Bella made her way to the edge of the room, her mind racing with thoughts of Hugh and the dangers he faced as a firefighter. She had always admired his bravery and dedication to his job, but now, faced with the reality of what that meant, she couldn't help but feel a sense of fear.

As the minutes ticked by, Bella found herself pacing back and forth, her eyes glued to the entrance of the community center. She couldn't shake the feeling that something was wrong, that Hugh was in trouble.

Just as she was about to give in to her fears and go looking for him, a figure appeared in the doorway. It was Hugh, his face smudged with soot and his hair disheveled. He looked exhausted, but there was a glimmer of triumph in his eyes.

Bella rushed towards him, her heart in her throat. "Hugh! Are you okay? What happened?"

He gave her a weary smile, pulling her into a tight hug. "We got the fire under control. Everyone's safe."

Bella clung to him, relief washing over her in waves. She buried her face in his chest, breathing in the scent of smoke and sweat that clung to his skin.

"I was so worried," she whispered, her voice muffled against his shirt. "I thought..."

Hugh pulled back, cupping her face in his hands. "I'm okay, Bella. I'm here."

He leaned in, his forehead resting against hers. Bella closed her eyes, savoring the feeling of his touch, the warmth of his breath on her skin before he finally pulled back, apologizing, "I'm so sorry, Bella. I'm a sooty mess, and I'm ruining your dress."

The last thing Bella cared about was her dress. She was just glad Hugh was okay. She smiled up at him. "What do you say we go grab a cup of hot cocoa from the diner?"

Hugh grinned back at her. "Sounds perfect."

Chapter Eleven

Bella awoke to a world blanketed in pure white, the first heavy snowfall of the season muffling the usual morning sounds. She shuffled to the window, her breath fogging the glass as she gazed out at the winter wonderland. The untouched expanse of snow brought a rush of memories—snow angels, sled races, and the unmistakable warmth of Hugh's laughter on those long-ago snow days.

She smiled wistfully, her heart aching for simpler times. Shaking off the nostalgia, she bundled up and headed out into the crisp morning air, her boots crunching through the fresh powder. As she rounded the corner, she caught sight of a familiar figure—Hugh, shoveling the sidewalk in front of the fire station, his cheeks ruddy from the cold.

"Morning, Bella!" he called out, his grin as bright as the snow. "Quite the winter welcome, huh?"

Bella laughed, the sound carrying across the quiet street. "It's like we're kids again, waking up to a snow day." She paused, a mischievous glint in her eye. "Remember that time we built a massive snow fort in your backyard?"

Hugh chuckled, leaning on his shovel. "How could I forget? We spent hours on that thing, and then your brother came along and knocked it down in seconds."

They both laughed at the shared memory, the years melting away. Hugh's smile softened. "Hey, I was just about to head over to Pinewood Farm to pick out the town's Christmas tree. Want to come along? For old times' sake?"

Bella hesitated for a moment, her thoughts torn between the pull of the past and the uncertainty of the present. But looking into Hugh's hopeful eyes, she found herself nodding. "I'd love to."

The scent of pine filled the air as Bella and Hugh wandered through the neat rows of Christmas trees at Pinewood Farm. The snow crunched beneath their feet, and the occasional burst of laughter from nearby families added to the festive atmosphere.

"What about this one?" Hugh asked, gesturing to a towering fir.

Bella tilted her head, considering. "It's nice, but I think we need something a bit fuller. Remember, it's got to be perfect for the town square."

They continued their search, the easy banter flowing between them as if no time had passed at all. As they rounded a corner, Bella spotted it—a magnificent spruce, its branches heavy with snow. "Hugh, look!" she exclaimed, hurrying over to the tree. "This is it. This is the one."

Hugh stood beside her, admiring the tree. His hand brushed against hers, sending a jolt of electricity through her gloved fingers. They turned to each other, eyes locking, the air suddenly charged with unspoken possibilities.

But the moment passed as quickly as it had come, both of them stepping back, the ghost of old fears and uncertainties whispering in the winter wind. They busied themselves with arranging for the tree's delivery, the magic of the moment slipping away like snowflakes on the breeze.

As they walked back to Hugh's truck, Bella couldn't help but wonder if she was letting her chance at happiness melt away, one hesitant step at a time. The snow continued to fall, blanketing the world in a hush, as if waiting for a decision to be made, a chance to be taken.

Chapter Twelve

Bella stepped into the warmth of the Pine Ridge Café, shaking the snow from her coat. As she made her way to the counter, a familiar voice called out, stopping her in her tracks.

"Bella, can I talk to you for a minute?" Rachel asked, her tone sweet but laced with an underlying edge.

Bella's heart sank, but she plastered on a smile. "Sure, Rachel. What's up?"

Rachel motioned for Bella to join her at a nearby table. As they sat down, Rachel leaned in, her eyes glinting with determination. "I just wanted to clear the air. About Hugh."

Bella's stomach twisted, but she kept her expression neutral. "What about him?"

"I know you two have history, but I think it's only fair that you know I'm still interested in him. I have been for a while now."

The words hit Bella like a punch to the gut. She swallowed hard, trying to compose herself. "I... I didn't realize..."

Rachel smiled, but it didn't quite reach her eyes. "I just thought you should know. I'd hate for there to be any misunderstandings."

Bella nodded, her mind reeling. "Of course. Thanks for telling me."

As Rachel left, Bella sat frozen, her thoughts spinning. She'd always known Hugh was a catch, but hearing Rachel's intentions out loud made it all too real. Suddenly, the café felt suffocating, the walls closing in around her.

She grabbed her coat and rushed out into the cold, her breath clouding in front of her. As she walked, she couldn't shake the nagging feeling of insecurity that Rachel's words had planted. Was she too late? Had she pushed Hugh away for good?

Meanwhile, across town, Hugh sat in his living

room, his head in his hands. His best friend, Jack, watched him with concern.

"I just don't know what to do," Hugh confessed, his voice strained. "Every time I think we're making progress, Bella pulls away again. It's like she's got these walls up, and I can't break through."

Jack sighed, leaning back in his chair. "Have you told her how you feel?"

Hugh shook his head. "Not in so many words. I'm afraid of scaring her off."

"But if you don't take that chance, you'll never know. You can't keep going on like this, man. It's eating you up inside."

Hugh knew Jack was right, but the thought of laying his heart on the line, only to have Bella reject him, was terrifying. He'd waited so long, hoping she'd come around on her own. But now, he wondered if he'd waited too long.

He stood up, pacing the room. "I just feel stuck, Jack. Like no matter what I do, I can't win."

Jack watched his friend, his heart aching for him. "You've got to talk to her, Hugh. Really talk to her. It's the only way."

Hugh stopped, staring out the window at the falling snow. He knew Jack was right. He couldn't keep living in this limbo, forever wondering what might have been. He had to take a chance, even if it meant risking everything.

With a heavy sigh, he grabbed his coat and headed for the door, determined to find Bella and lay his cards on the table, once and for all.

Bella trudged through the snow-covered streets of Pine Ridge, her boots leaving deep imprints in the fresh powder. The cold wind nipped at her cheeks, but she barely noticed, too lost in her own thoughts to care.

She'd always prided herself on her independence, on her ability to forge her own path and chase her dreams. But now, faced with the possibility of a future with Hugh, she found herself faltering.

It wasn't that she didn't care for him. She did, more than she'd ever admitted to anyone, even herself. But the thought of opening up, of letting herself be vulnerable, terrified her.

She'd been hurt before, had her heart broken into a million pieces. And she'd sworn she'd never let it happen again. But now, with Hugh, she wondered if she was letting her fear hold her back from something truly special.

Bella stopped, staring up at the twinkling lights that adorned the town square. She remembered standing in this very spot with Hugh, years ago, watching the Christmas tree lighting ceremony. They'd been so young then, so full of hope and possibility.

She shook her head, trying to clear the memories from her mind. But they persisted, swirling around her like the snowflakes that danced on the breeze.

"What am I doing?" she whispered to herself, her breath fogging in the cold air. "Why am I running from the one thing I've always wanted?"

She thought of Rachel, of the way she'd looked at Hugh, the desire clear in her eyes. And she felt a pang of jealousy, sharp and unexpected.

But it wasn't just jealousy. It was fear, too. Fear that if she didn't act soon, she'd lose Hugh forever. And the thought of that was more painful than anything she'd ever experienced.

Bella closed her eyes, taking a deep breath. She thought of Rachel and how she'd made her intentions clear, and her heart gave a pang. Would she be breaking some sacred girl code to go after Hugh now?

She didn't know what to do.

Chapter Thirteen

Bella stood in the center of the town square, a clipboard clutched to her chest as she directed volunteers sorting through piles of donated gifts. The crisp December air nipped at her cheeks, but the warmth of the community coming together filled her heart.

"Hey there, need an extra pair of hands?" A familiar voice called out. Bella turned to see Hugh approaching, his signature smile lighting up his face.

"Hugh! I didn't expect to see you here," Bella said, surprise coloring her tone. "Aren't you on call today?"

"Nah, switched shifts with Jenkins. Figured this was more important." He gestured to the bustling activity around them. "You're doing an amazing thing here, Bells."

She felt a flush creep up her neck at the praise and the use of his old nickname for her. "It's not just me. It's everyone coming together, making sure no child goes without a gift this Christmas."

Hugh nodded, his gaze filled with admiration. "True, but it takes a special someone to rally the troops like this. Mind if I join in?"

"Of course not! We can always use more help." Bella handed him a stack of gift tags. "You can start by matching these to the presents."

As they worked side by side, laughing and chatting with the other volunteers, Bella couldn't help but steal glances at Hugh. The way he joked with the elderly Mrs. Peterson, or how he carefully selected just the right gift for each child—it reminded her of the thoughtful, caring man she'd fallen for years ago.

But so much had changed since then. She had her life in New York, her career. Hugh's world revolved around Pine Ridge. Could they really find a way to bridge that gap?

"Earth to Bella," Hugh teased, waving a hand in front of her face. "Where'd you go just now?"

She shook her head, dispelling the thoughts.

"Sorry, just mentally running through my checklist. Making sure we haven't missed anything."

Hugh placed a gentle hand on her shoulder. "Hey, it's perfect. You've done an incredible job here. These kids are going to have the best Christmas, thanks to you."

Bella met his gaze, her heart skipping a beat at the sincerity she found there. "Thanks to all of us," she corrected softly.

As they held each other's eyes, Bella felt a flicker of something she'd thought long extinguished. A connection, a spark. But before she could examine it further, a volunteer called out to her with a question, and the moment was broken.

They returned to their tasks, the air between them filled with unspoken words and remembered feelings. And though they worked alongside one another for hours, Bella sensed they were both holding back, unsure of how to cross the chasm of time and distance that separated them.

As the day drew to a close, Bella and Hugh found themselves standing outside the community center, the last of the gifts delivered. The winter air was crisp, and the sky had taken on a soft, gray hue that hinted at the possibility of snow.

Bella pulled her coat tighter around her, savoring the feeling of accomplishment that came with a job well done. She turned to Hugh, a smile playing at the corners of her mouth. "I can't believe we did it. Every single gift, delivered."

Hugh grinned back at her, his blue eyes sparkling with warmth. "I never doubted it for a second. Not with you at the helm."

A comfortable silence settled between them as they watched their breath mist in the cold air. Bella's mind drifted to the donation Hugh had made, the way he'd quietly stepped in to help without seeking recognition. It was so like him, so quintessentially Hugh.

She was about to mention it when something caught her eye. There, hanging above the doorway of the community center, was a sprig of mistletoe. Bella's heart stuttered in her chest. Surely, it hadn't been there earlier?

Hugh followed her gaze, and a flicker of surprise crossed his features. Then, slowly, he turned back to her, his expression unreadable.

Bella swallowed hard, suddenly hyper-aware of

how close they were standing. The air between them felt charged, electric with possibility.

"Mistletoe," Hugh murmured, his voice low and husky. "You know what that means."

Bella's pulse raced as Hugh took a step closer, his hand coming up to cup her cheek. His touch was gentle, almost reverent, and Bella found herself leaning into it, her eyes fluttering closed.

When his lips met hers, it was like coming home. The kiss was soft, tentative at first, but it quickly deepened as years of pent-up longing poured out between them. Bella's hands fisted in the front of Hugh's coat, pulling him closer, while his arms encircled her waist, holding her tight against him.

As the first flakes of snow began to fall around them, Bella lost herself in the kiss, in the feeling of being in Hugh's arms once more. For a moment, the years fell away, and they were just Bella and Hugh, two hearts finding their way back to each other.

But even as she surrendered to the magic of the moment, a small voice in the back of Bella's mind whispered a warning. This wasn't part of the plan. She had a life waiting for her back in New York, a career she'd worked so hard to build.

Could she really risk it all for a second chance at love?

Bella pulled back, her breath coming in short puffs that mingled with the chilly air. She searched Hugh's face, taking in the swirl of emotions in his eyes—hope, longing, and a touch of uncertainty.

"Hugh, I..." She trailed off, unsure of what to say. Her heart was telling her one thing, but her head was saying another. "I don't know if I can do this."

Hugh's brow furrowed, his hands still resting on her waist. "Bella, I know we have a lot to figure out, but doesn't this feel right to you?"

She closed her eyes, trying to gather her thoughts. Of course, it felt right. Being in Hugh's arms, kissing him under the falling snow—it was like something out of a dream. But the reality was that she had a life in New York, one she'd worked so hard to build.

"It's not that simple," Bella said, her voice barely above a whisper. "I have responsibilities, commitments. I can't just walk away from everything."

Hugh's grip on her tightened, as if he was afraid she might slip away. "I'm not asking you to walk away, Bella. I'm just asking for a chance."

Bella's heart clenched at the raw emotion in his voice. She knew he meant every word, but the doubts still lingered. What if they tried again and it didn't work out? What if she gave up everything for a love that was never meant to be?

"I need time," she said, her voice trembling slightly. "Time to think, to figure out what I want."

Hugh nodded, his expression a mix of understanding and disappointment. "I get it, Bella. Take all the time you need." He pressed a gentle kiss to her forehead. "Just know that I'll be here, waiting for you."

As they walked back to the community center in silence, Bella's mind raced with conflicting thoughts and emotions. The kiss had awakened something in her, a longing she'd tried so hard to bury.

But was she ready to risk everything?

Chapter Fourteen

Bella stood in the center of the town square, her breath forming clouds in the chilly December air. She surveyed the half-decorated Christmas tree, the unlit street lamps, and the bare wooden stalls waiting to be filled with festive vendors. Her checklist felt a mile long.

"Need some help?" Hugh's deep voice startled her from behind. Bella spun around, nearly dropping her clipboard. He looked devastatingly handsome in his firefighter uniform, as usual.

"Oh, hi Hugh. I'm just...trying to get everything finalized for the Christmas Eve festival tomorrow." She tucked a loose strand of hair behind her ear, flustered by his sudden appearance and easy smile.

Hugh stepped closer, his blue eyes twinkling.

"Looks like you could use an extra pair of hands. Why don't you let me help string up those lights?" He gestured to the tangled strands piled nearby.

Bella hesitated, biting her lower lip. Having Hugh around both thrilled and terrified her. The way he looked at her stirred up feelings she'd long buried. "I wouldn't want to impose. I'm sure you're busy with work..."

"Nonsense." Hugh waved off her protest. "For you, I've got all the time in the world." He winked, sending her heart fluttering.

Together, they began draping twinkling lights around the towering spruce tree. As they worked, their gloved hands brushed, sending sparks through Bella that had nothing to do with electricity. She couldn't meet his gaze, afraid he'd see the longing she'd tried so hard to hide.

As soon as they finished, Hugh got a work call and rushed off to be the hero again.

With a heavy sigh, Bella turned and made her way to the cozy café where she was meeting Chloe. As she stepped inside, the warmth and the aroma of freshly brewed coffee enveloped her. Chloe waved from a corner table, her eyes filled with concern.

"Hey, sis," Chloe said as Bella sat down. "You

look like you've got the weight of the world on your shoulders."

Bella wrapped her hands around the steaming mug of coffee Chloe had ordered for her. "I feel like I'm at a crossroads, Chlo."

Chloe reached across the table and squeezed Bella's hand. "Sis, I know you've been through a lot, but you can't let fear control your life. What does your heart tell you?"

"My heart..." Bella closed her eyes, picturing Hugh's warm smile and the way he made her feel cherished. "My heart wants something I'm afraid to have."

"Then maybe it's time to listen to it," Chloe said gently. "You've worked so hard to build your career, but don't forget to leave room for love. You deserve to be happy, Bella."

Bella felt tears prickling behind her eyelids. Deep down, she knew Chloe was right. She had been so focused on her professional goals that she had neglected her own happiness.

"I'm scared, Chlo," she whispered. "But I think I'm more scared of losing Hugh forever."

Chloe smiled, her eyes shining with understanding. "Then you've got to make a choice."

❄

Bella stood by the frost-covered window of her childhood bedroom, watching the snowflakes dance and swirl in the wind. The soft glow of the Christmas lights from the festival preparations cast a warm, inviting shine across the town square. Despite the picturesque scene, her heart felt heavy with the weight of the decision she knew she had to make.

She thought back to her conversation with Chloe, her sister's words echoing in her mind. "You have to decide what will make you truly happy, Bella. Don't let fear hold you back from the life you deserve."

Bella sighed, her breath fogging the glass. She had always been so sure of her path, so focused on her career and the life she had built in New York City. But standing here, in the quiet stillness of her hometown, she realized that perhaps the life she thought she wanted wasn't the one that would bring her true joy.

Her gaze drifted to the framed photograph on her nightstand—a candid shot of her and Hugh, laughing together at a high school football game. The warmth in his eyes, the genuine affection in his smile... it was a stark contrast to the emotional distance that had grown between them in recent days.

Bella's heart ached at the thought of losing him, of letting her fears and doubts rob her of a chance at real happiness. She knew she had to make a choice, to take a leap of faith and trust in the love they shared.

With a newfound sense of resolve, Bella turned from the window and reached for her coat. It was time to stop running from her feelings and embrace the possibility of a future with Hugh. She only hoped it wasn't too late.

As she stepped out into the snow-covered streets, Bella felt a flutter of nervousness in her stomach. But beneath it all, there was a glimmer of hope, a whisper of the love she knew she couldn't deny any longer. With each step, she moved closer to the life she truly wanted, ready to face whatever challenges lay ahead —as long as Hugh was by her side.

Chapter Fifteen

The sounds of laughter and Christmas carols filled the frosty evening air as string lights twinkled above the bustling festival square. Bella stood at the edge of the crowd, her eyes scanning the sea of smiling faces and festive decorations. She breathed in the scent of cinnamon and pine, a wistful smile playing on her lips.

Despite the joy surrounding her, a heaviness weighed on Bella's heart. Seeing Hugh again after all these years had stirred up feelings she thought were long buried. As she watched couples strolling hand-in-hand beneath the glimmering lights, she couldn't help but wonder what could have been.

"Penny for your thoughts?" Hugh's warm voice cut through her reverie.

Bella turned to find him standing beside her, his blue eyes crinkling at the corners as he smiled. "Just admiring how everything turned out. The festival is a hit."

"All thanks to your hard work and vision." Hugh placed a gentle hand on her shoulder. "But I can tell something's on your mind. Walk with me?"

Nodding, Bella fell into step beside him as they wove through the crowd. The crunch of snow beneath their boots mingled with the distant sounds of the festival.

"I have a surprise for you," Hugh said, leading her towards a quieter corner of the square.

There, nestled among the evergreens, stood a small Christmas tree adorned with an eclectic array of ornaments. Bella's breath caught as she stepped closer, recognizing each one.

"Is that...?"

"The friendship bracelet you made me in third grade," Hugh confirmed, pointing to a braided loop. "And there's the ticket stub from our first school dance."

Bella reached out to touch a delicate glass baseball. "From when you hit that home run to win the championship senior year."

As she examined each ornament, memories of

their shared history washed over her. Hugh had saved every small token of their friendship, their childhood, their...almost. Bella blinked back the sudden sting of tears.

"I wanted you to know," Hugh said softly, "that no matter how much time has passed, you've always been an important part of my life, Bells. Every step of the way."

Bella met his gaze, saw the sincerity and warmth shining in his eyes. Her heart swelled with a longing she could no longer ignore. But the weight of their history, the fear of risking their friendship, still held her back.

She managed a shaky smile. "I don't know what to say, Hugh. This is...it means so much."

He reached out to tuck a stray lock of hair behind her ear, his fingers lingering against her cheek. "You don't have to say anything. I just wanted you to know."

As they stood there, the rest of the world fading away, Bella knew she had a choice to make. She could cling to the safety of the past, or take a leap of faith into an uncertain future.

Bella took a deep breath, steeling herself for the words she'd held back for so long. "Hugh, I...I need to tell you something."

He tilted his head, concern etching his features. "What is it, Bells?"

"I've been running from my feelings for years, afraid of what it might mean for us. But seeing all of this," she gestured to the ornaments, "I realize that my love for you has never faded. I'm scared, Hugh, but I don't want to run anymore."

Hugh's eyes widened, a flicker of hope igniting within them. He grasped her hands, his touch gentle yet reassuring. "Bella, I've loved you since we were kids. I've just been waiting for the right moment to tell you."

A tearful laugh escaped her lips. "We've wasted so much time, haven't we?"

He shook his head, a soft smile playing on his lips. "No, we've been growing, learning, becoming the people we needed to be. And now, here we are, exactly where we're meant to be."

With their truths laid bare, Bella and Hugh embraced, years of pent-up emotion pouring into the simple act. As they pulled apart, Hugh's gaze drifted to the festival crowd, a mischievous glint in his eye.

"What do you say we make this official?"

Before Bella could respond, Hugh turned to face the gathered townspeople, his voice ringing out clear and strong. "Excuse me, everyone! I have something I need to say."

Curious faces turned their way, and Bella felt her cheeks warm as Hugh continued, "I've been in love with Bella York since I was ten years old. She's always been the one for me, no matter how much time has passed. And I don't want to waste another moment without her knowing that."

A chorus of aww's and cheers erupted from the crowd, and Bella found herself laughing and crying all at once. She stepped forward, lacing her fingers with Hugh's and burying her head against his shoulder.

The cheers and applause from the crowd filled the air as Bella and Hugh stood hand in hand, their hearts overflowing with the joy of their newfound love. The twinkling lights of the Christmas tree cast a warm, magical glow over the scene, making the moment feel like something straight out of a fairytale.

Bella gazed up at Hugh, her eyes shining with happy tears. "I can't believe this is really happening," she whispered, her voice barely audible above the celebratory noise.

Hugh smiled down at her, his expression soft and tender. "Believe it, darlin'," he murmured, brushing a stray lock of hair from her face. "This is just the beginning of our forever."

As the festival began to wind down, friends and family members approached the couple, offering their congratulations and well-wishes. Bella and Hugh accepted each hug and handshake with gratitude, their hearts full to bursting with the love and support of their community.

Finally, as the last of the crowd dispersed, Hugh turned to Bella with a mischievous grin. "What do you say we get out of here and start celebrating, just the two of us?"

Bella laughed, her eyes sparkling with anticipation. "I thought you'd never ask."

Hand in hand, they walked away from the festival grounds, the sounds of music and laughter fading behind them. The future stretched out before them, bright and full of promise, and they knew that whatever challenges lay ahead, they would face them together.

As they disappeared into the night, the Christmas tree stood tall and proud, its lights twinkling like a beacon of hope and love. And in that moment, everyone who had witnessed Bella and Hugh's story knew that sometimes, the greatest gifts of all were the ones that came straight from the heart.

Chapter Sixteen

Bella awoke to the gentle touch of sunlight on her face, filtering through the lace curtains of her childhood bedroom. The comforting scent of cinnamon rolls wafted up from the kitchen below, enveloping her in warmth and nostalgia. She stretched languidly, a smile playing on her lips as realization dawned—it was Christmas morning, and for the first time in years, she felt truly at peace.

Slipping out of bed, Bella padded downstairs, following the joyful chatter and laughter emanating from the living room. As she entered, Hugh looked up from his spot on the couch, his blue eyes sparkling with affection. How very perfect that he was already here. "Merry Christmas, Bella," he said softly, patting the space beside him.

Bella smiled, her heart swelling with happiness as she settled next to him. "Merry Christmas, Hugh." She leaned into his embrace, savoring the comfort and security of his presence.

Around them, Bella's family bustled about, exchanging gifts and sharing stories. Her mother, aproned and beaming, pressed a steaming mug of hot cocoa into Bella's hands. "It's so good to have you home, sweetheart," she murmured, planting a gentle kiss on Bella's forehead.

As the morning unfolded, Bella found herself increasingly content, surrounded by the love and warmth of her family and the man who had captured her heart. She laughed at her father's corny jokes, helped her little sister unwrap presents, and sneaked glances at Hugh, marveling at how perfectly he fit into her world.

Later, as they sat together on the porch swing, watching snowflakes drift lazily from the sky, Hugh turned to Bella, his expression earnest. "I've been thinking," he began, taking her hand in his. "What if we built a life together here, in Pine Ridge? I know it's not New York, but it's home. And I want to make a home with you, Bella."

Bella's breath caught in her throat, her eyes welling with happy tears. In that moment, she knew with absolute certainty that this was where she belonged—in the arms of the man she loved, in the town that had shaped her. "Yes," she whispered, leaning in to capture his lips in a tender kiss. "Let's make a home together, right here in Pine Ridge."

As they held each other close, their hearts brimming with joy and anticipation for the future, Bella realized that she had found the greatest gift of all—the promise of a lifetime of love and happiness, right where she was meant to be.

The shrill ring of Bella's phone interrupted the peaceful moment. She glanced at the screen, surprised to see her New York client's name flashing insistently. With an apologetic smile to Hugh, she stepped inside to take the call.

"Bella, darling!" the client's voice boomed through the receiver. "I hope you've enjoyed your little holiday, but it's time to come back to the real world. I have a massive event coming up, and I need your expertise. When can you be back in the city?"

Bella hesitated, her gaze drifting to the window where she could see Hugh waiting patiently on the porch swing. The life she had built in New York suddenly felt distant, like a half-remembered dream.

"I'm sorry, but I won't be returning to New York," she said, the words tumbling out before she could second-guess herself. "My priorities have changed, and I've realized that my place is here, in Pine Ridge."

The client spluttered in disbelief, but Bella held firm, a smile playing at the corners of her mouth as she ended the call. She stepped back outside, the crisp winter air filling her lungs as she settled beside Hugh once more.

"Everything okay?" he asked, concern etched in his handsome features.

Bella nodded, her heart swelling with certainty. "Everything is perfect," she murmured, lacing her fingers with his. "I just turned down a job offer in New York. I'm staying right here, where I belong."

Hugh's eyes widened in surprise, then crinkled with joy as he pulled her close. "Do you know how good it feels to hear you say that?"

"About as good as it feels to say it, I imagine," Bella said, her gaze sweeping over the quaint houses, the twinkling Christmas lights, and the familiar faces of her loved ones. "This is where I'm meant to be, Hugh. Here, with you, surrounded by the people and the place that make me feel whole."

As the sun began to set, casting a golden glow over the snowy landscape, Bella snuggled closer to

Hugh, a sense of peace and contentment washing over her. She had finally found her way home, not just to Pine Ridge, but to the life she was always meant to live. And as she looked up at the man who held her heart, she knew that this was just the beginning of a beautiful future together.

Hugh turned to face Bella, taking her hands in his, his blue eyes shimmering with emotion.

"Bella," he began, his voice soft and earnest, "being with you these past few weeks has made me realize that I don't want to spend another day without you by my side."

Bella's breath caught in her throat as Hugh slowly lowered himself to one knee, the snow crunching beneath him. He pulled a box from his pocket and opened it, revealing a simple yet elegant diamond ring that sparkled in the fading light.

"I know I'm just a small-town firefighter, and I may not have much to offer, but I promise to love you with all my heart, every single day, for the rest of our lives." His voice trembled with emotion as he continued, "Bella York, will you marry me?"

Tears of joy streamed down Bella's face as she nodded, her words catching in her throat. "Yes," she managed to whisper, her heart bursting with love and happiness. "Yes, Hugh, I will marry you."

Hugh slipped the ring onto her finger, his own eyes glistening with tears as he rose to his feet and pulled her into a tender embrace. Their lips met in a kiss that held the promise of a lifetime together, the warmth of their love shielding them from the winter chill.

As they parted, Bella looked up at Hugh's eyes crinkled with happiness, and her heart melted. In that moment, she knew that she had found more than just a home in Pine Ridge—she had found her soulmate, her partner in life, and the key to her happily ever after.

The twinkling lights of the Christmas tree blurred as Cassie blinked back tears, a flute of untouched champagne in her hand. Laughter and chatter filled the air, but she felt disconnected from it all, an outsider looking in.

She sighed and glanced at her watch. Only an hour until she could slip away unnoticed. Being single at a holiday party was the worst—happy couples everywhere only reminded her of what she didn't have.

"Cassie, there you are!" Her colleague Mindy appeared, cheeks flushed from the festivities. "Come join the gift exchange. We're about to start."

Cassie forced a smile. "Thanks, but I think I'll sit

this one out. I'm not really in the Christmas spirit this year."

Mindy's brow furrowed in concern. "Is everything okay? You've seemed down lately."

Before Cassie could deflect, her cell phone buzzed in her clutch. She fished it out, relieved for the distraction. "Sorry, I need to take this. Excuse me."

She stepped into a quiet corner and answered. "Hello?"

"Cassie! It's Emily." Her sister's cheery voice filled the line. "I'm so glad I caught you. Listen, are you coming home for Christmas? Aunt Mae is hosting her usual holiday bash on Christmas Eve and the whole town will be there. It wouldn't be the same without you."

Cassie hesitated. Christmas in her cozy hometown sounded idyllic...and utterly exhausting in her current state. "I don't know, Em. Work has been crazy and I'm just not feeling very festive this year."

"All the more reason to come!" Emily insisted. "You've been working too hard. Come back to your roots, recharge, remember what the holidays are really about. We all miss you."

Cassie's throat tightened. She did miss her family. And maybe a dose of small-town charm was exactly what she needed to heal her bruised heart. "Okay," she relented. "I'll be there."

"Yes! I can't wait to see you." Emily's grin was audible through the phone. "It's going to be the best Christmas yet, I just know it. Love you!"

"Love you too." Cassie ended the call, a spark of something like hope flickering in her chest. She glanced around the party, suddenly feeling lighter.

Perhaps this year, she'd find her lost love for the holidays again. All she needed was to go home. She said a quick prayer for guidance, and then felt a peace settle over her that let her know going home was exactly what she was supposed to do.

Cassie surveyed her suitcase, mentally ticking off her packing list. Thick sweaters, warm socks, her coziest pajamas—everything she'd need for a winter getaway in the Carolinas. She zipped the luggage shut with a sigh, still not entirely convinced this trip was a good idea.

"It's just for a few days," she reminded herself aloud, her voice echoing in the emptiness of her Atlanta apartment. "A little holiday cheer never hurt anyone, right?"

But as she loaded her bags into the car and set off down the highway, Cassie couldn't shake the lingering uncertainty. She'd spent so long building her career, she'd almost forgotten how to simply enjoy life. Could a few days in her hometown really change that?

Miles melted away beneath her tires, the city giving way to rolling hills and dense forests. The farther she drove, the more the landscape transformed into a winter wonderland. Snow blanketed the ground, clinging to the branches of towering evergreens. The air seemed to sparkle with a crisp, magical quality.

By the time Cassie turned onto the familiar winding road leading to Aunt Mae's bed-and-breakfast, she felt like she'd stepped into a Hallmark movie. The Victorian-style house looked like something from a postcard, with its wraparound porch and gabled roof. Twinkling lights adorned every eave and railing, casting a warm glow over the freshly fallen snow.

Cassie parked her car and took a moment to breathe in the scene. The air smelled of pine and wood smoke, inviting and nostalgic. In the distance, she could hear the faint strains of Christmas carols and the laughter of children playing in the snow.

"I'm really here," she whispered, a smile tugging at her lips. "Maybe this was a good idea after all."

With renewed energy, Cassie grabbed her bags and made her way up the porch steps. The door flew open before she could even knock, revealing the beaming face of her Aunt Mae.

"Cassie, darling! You made it!" Mae enveloped her in a warm hug that smelled of cinnamon and spice. "Come in, come in! Let's get you settled. Christmas just isn't Christmas until the whole family is together."

As Cassie stepped over the threshold into the warmth and cheer of the bed-and-breakfast, she felt a piece of her heart slip back into place. This was exactly where she needed to be.

Mae led Cassie into the cozy foyer, its walls adorned with garlands and vintage Christmas decorations. "I've got you in your usual room upstairs, honey. I hope you don't mind, but we're fully booked this year! Seems like everyone wants a taste of small-town Christmas magic."

Cassie smiled, shrugging off her coat. "I don't mind at all, Aunt Mae. I'm just happy to be here. It's been too long."

As she turned to hang her coat on the rack, Cassie's eyes caught on a tall figure emerging from the living room. He was handsome, with auburn hair and a warmth in his eyes that seemed to match the glow of the Christmas lights.

But he was in and out before she got a chance to catch his name.

"Why don't you head on up and get settled in and I'll make us some of my famous hot cocoa?" Her aunt broke into her thoughts.

Cassie thought of how good a shower would be and smiled at her aunt. "That sounds lovely."

About the Author

Award-winning author Kayla Lowe writes women's fiction that explores complex themes with sensitivity and depth. Kayla's books delve into the intricacies of relationships, self-discovery, and resilience. From cozy love stories interspersed with a bit of faith to heartwarming tales of friendship and suspenseful novels of empowerment and heartbreak, her books illustrate the struggles specific to women.

When she's not churning out her next novel, you can find her with her feet in the sand and a book in her hand or curled up on the couch with her dogs.

Visit her website at www.authorkaylalowe.com.

A Courtship in Covent Garden

Whispers in Westminster

Romance in Regent's Park

Serenade on Strand Street

Treasure in Tower Bridge

<u>Sweet Honey by the Sea</u>

<u>The Beekeeper's Secret (Book 1)</u>

<u>A Royal Honeycomb (Book 2)</u>

<u>Bees in Blossom (Book 3)</u>

<u>Honeyed Kisses (Book 4)</u>

<u>Blooming Forever (Book 5)</u>

<u>Strawberry Beach Series</u>

<u>Beachside Lessons (Book 1)</u>

<u>Beachside Lessons (Book 2)</u>

<u>Beachside Lessons (Book 3)</u>

Panama City Beach Series

Sun-Kissed Secrets (Book 1)

Sun-Kissed Secrets (Book 2)

Sun-Kissed Secrets (Book 3)

The Tainted Love Saga

Of Love and Deception (Book 1)

Of Love and Family (Book 2)

Of Love and Violence (Book 3)

Of Love and Abuse(Book 4)

Of Love and Crime (Book 5)

Of Love and Addiction (Book 6)

Of Love and Redemption (Book 7)

<u>Standalones</u>

Maiden's Blush

<u>Poetry</u>

Phantom Poetry

Lost and Found